# A message from the Sleep Health Foundation

**Some children have trouble going to sleep. What can you do?**

Sleep is one of the most important things a human can do every day. Experts agree that children aged 1–2 years generally need 11–14 hours of sleep across a 24 hour period. Those aged 3–5 years should be getting 10–13 hours.

But, so many children find getting to sleep difficult. The Sleep Health Foundation has a range of helpful fact sheets that deal with behavioural issues around bedtime, sleep in general and for children with particular sleep problems. These include tips on sleep issues for children with ADHD or autism, as well as more general topics such as bedwetting, nightmares, sleep terrors and childhood snoring.

There are also tips at the back of this book to encourage a healthy sleep pattern in children from an early age.

**For more information, visit:** https://www.sleephealthfoundation.org.au

# The Wiggles

# The Bedtime Book

Scan the code to sing
along to the story!

SCAN ME

Well, the night has come around again,
it's time to go to bed.

There are things you have to do,
before you rest your weary head.

First, you need to have a bath.
Use soap so that you're nice and clean.

And, make sure you wash behind your ears, to sleep and dream.

Some pyjamas you'll put on.

And then your teeth you will brush.

Now, go to the toilet,

and don't forget to flush!

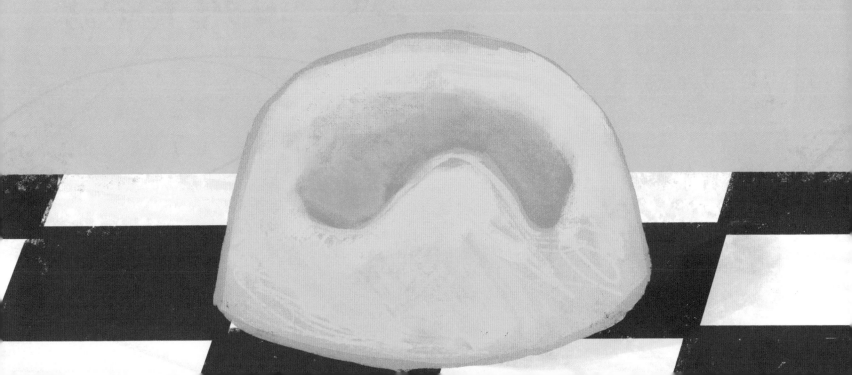

Read a book, a bedtime story.

That's before you say goodnight.

With a yawn, it's time to sleep.

And please, turn out the light!

Well, can you remember what I said?

The things to do before it's bed?

When someone says again,

again, it's time for bed.

It's time for bed.

**1** Have a bath.

**2** Put on pyjamas.

**3** Brush your teeth.

**4** Go to the toilet.

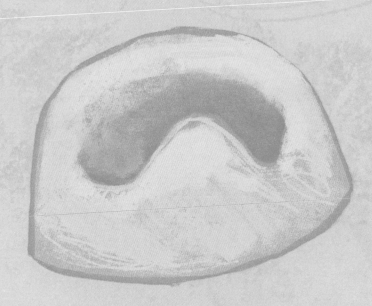

**5** Read a book.

**6** You say goodnight.

**7** Turn out the light!

So, when someone says again, again,

it's time for bed. It's time for bed!

Now you know what you should do,

before it's bed.

before it's bed.

# 1 Have a bath.

**2** Put on pyjamas.

**3** Brush your teeth.

**4** Go to the toilet.

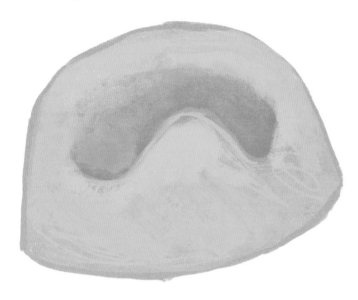

**5** Read a book.

**6** You say goodnight.

**7** Turn out the light.

# Helpful tips from the Sleep Health Foundation

### 1. Establish a regular sleep pattern
Regular hours of sleep are important. It will help your child understand when it is time to sleep.  Also, your child will have better sleep. Bedtime shouldn't vary by more than an hour across all days of the week – whether your child has an early start the next morning or not. The same goes for getting up time.

### 2. A consistent bedtime routine
It is good to have the same routine before bed each night. This will help prepare for sleep. Quiet activities are good – such as being read to, singing quiet songs together or having a bath or shower. In the half hour before bed, there are some things you don't want your child to do. These are more active games, playing outside, watching TV or playing internet games.

### 3. Make sure the bedroom is comfortable
The bedroom should be quiet, comfortable and as dark as possible. Some children like a night light. This is fine. Make sure your child sees the bedroom as a good place to be. You can help do this by not using it as a place for punishment.

Taking a comfort object to bed, like a teddy bear, can help your child feel less alone at night. If they seem anxious, reassure them that nothing will hurt them. Sometimes, a baby monitor in their room (linked to you) will help.